Dear Parents and Educators,

Welcome to Penguin Young Readers! As parents and educators, you know that each child develops at his or her own pace—in terms of speech, critical thinking, and, of course, reading. Penguin Young Readers recognizes this fact. As a result, each Penguin Young Readers book is assigned a traditional easy-to-read level (1–4) as well as a Guided Reading Level (A–P). Both of these systems will help you choose the right book for your child. Please refer to the back of each book for specific leveling information. Penguin Young Readers features esteemed authors and illustrators, stories about favorite characters, fascinating nonfiction, and more!

Turtle and Snake Go Camping

LEVEL 1

GUIDED READING LEVEL **D**

This book is perfect for an **Emergent Reader** who:
- can read in a left-to-right and top-to-bottom progression;
- can recognize some beginning and ending letter sounds;
- can use picture clues to help tell the story; and
- can understand the basic plot and sequence of simple stories.

Here are some **activities** you can do during and after reading this book:
- Picture Clues: Go through the book and match the pictures to the words. For example, have the child point to the picture of the tent, and then read the word *tent* in the story.
- Word Repetition: Find and read all the words that are repeated in the story. For example, *splash, splash*. How many times is this phrase used?
- Retelling: Have the child tell you what the story is about.

Remember, sharing the love of reading with a child is the best gift you can give!

—Bonnie Bader, EdM, and Katie Carella, EdM
  Penguin Young Readers program

*Penguin Young Readers are leveled by independent reviewers applying the standards developed by Irene Fountas and Gay Su Pinnell in *Matching Books to Readers: Using Leveled Books in Guided Reading*, Heinemann, 1999.

To all the great libraries and
librarians, and to the kids
who find their adventures there—KS

Penguin Young Readers
Published by the Penguin Group
Penguin Group (USA) Inc., 375 Hudson Street, New York, New York 10014, USA
Penguin Group (Canada), 90 Eglinton Avenue East, Suite 700, Toronto, Ontario M4P 2Y3, Canada
(a division of Pearson Penguin Canada Inc.)
Penguin Books Ltd., 80 Strand, London WC2R 0RL, England
Penguin Group Ireland, 25 St. Stephen's Green, Dublin 2, Ireland (a division of Penguin Books Ltd.)
Penguin Group (Australia), 250 Camberwell Road, Camberwell, Victoria 3124, Australia
(a division of Pearson Australia Group Pty. Ltd.)
Penguin Books India Pvt. Ltd., 11 Community Centre, Panchsheel Park, New Delhi—110 017, India
Penguin Group (NZ), 67 Apollo Drive, Rosedale, Auckland 0632, New Zealand
(a division of Pearson New Zealand Ltd.)
Penguin Books (South Africa) (Pty.) Ltd., 24 Sturdee Avenue,
Rosebank, Johannesburg 2196, South Africa

Penguin Books Ltd., Registered Offices: 80 Strand, London WC2R 0RL, England

Library of Congress Control Number: 99057508

ISBN 978-0-14-130670-4   1 0 9 8 7 6

Turtle and Snake Go Camping

by Kate Spohn

WITHDRAWN

Penguin Young Readers
An Imprint of Penguin Group (USA) Inc.

Let's go camping!

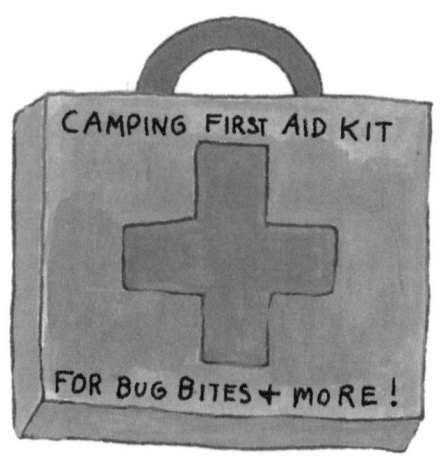

Pack the tent.

Pack the sleeping bags.

Pack the food.

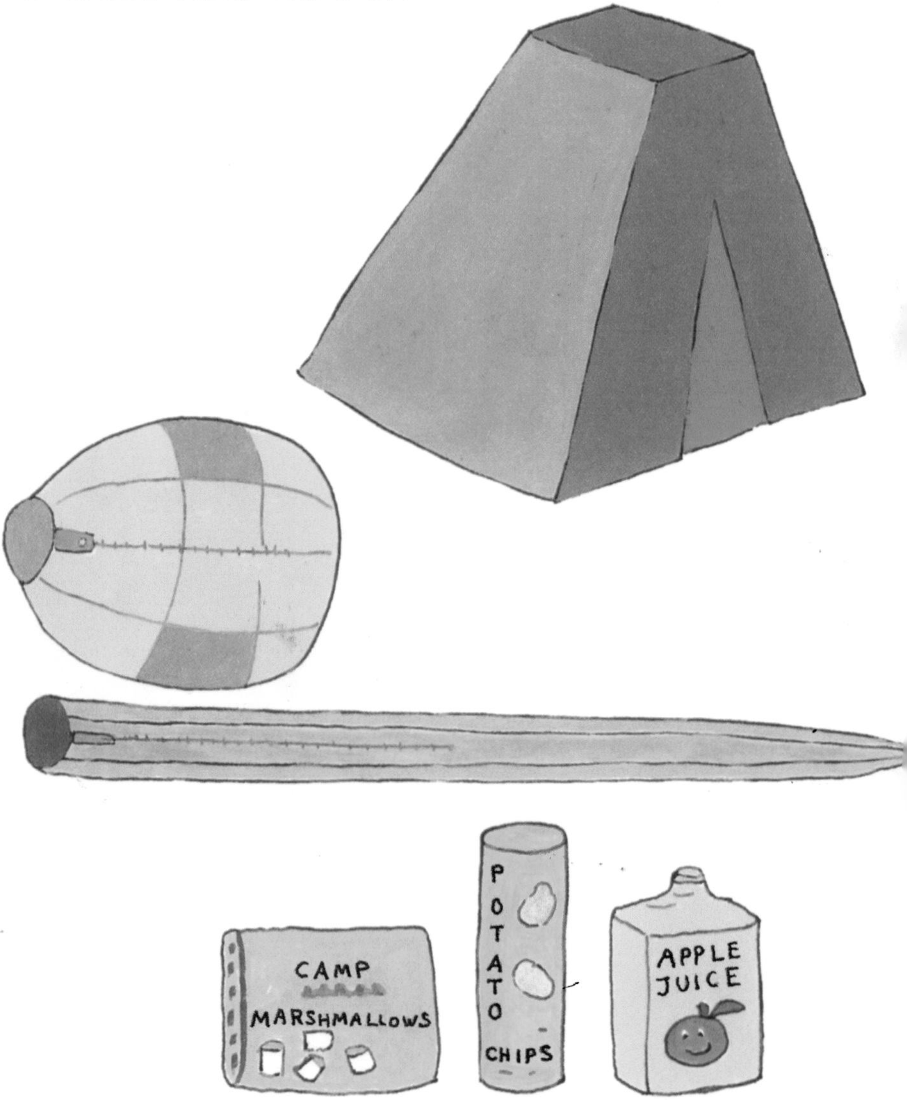

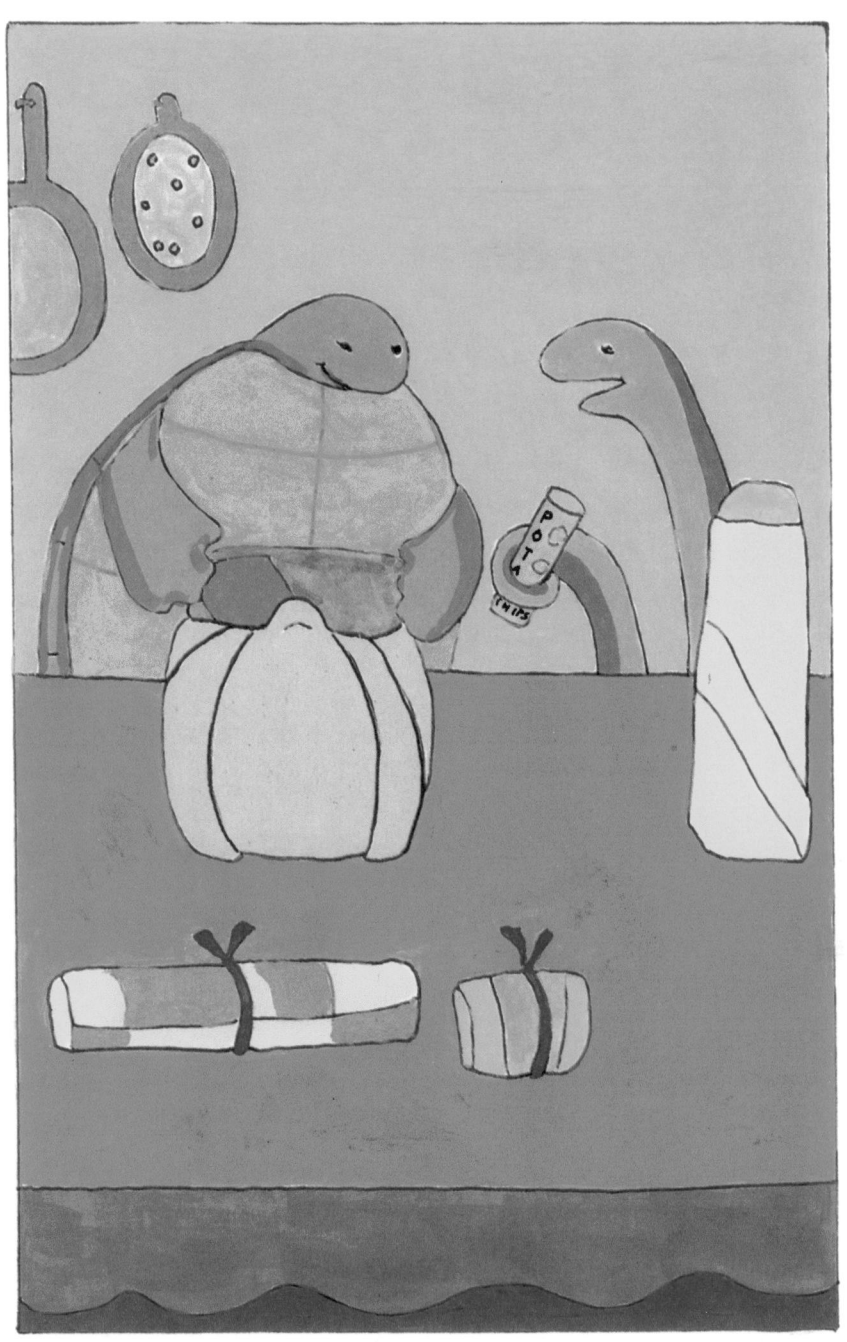

March, march
around the trees.

Splash, splash

in the brook.

Row, row across the pond.

There it is.

A perfect spot to camp.

Up goes the tent.

Down go the sleeping bags.

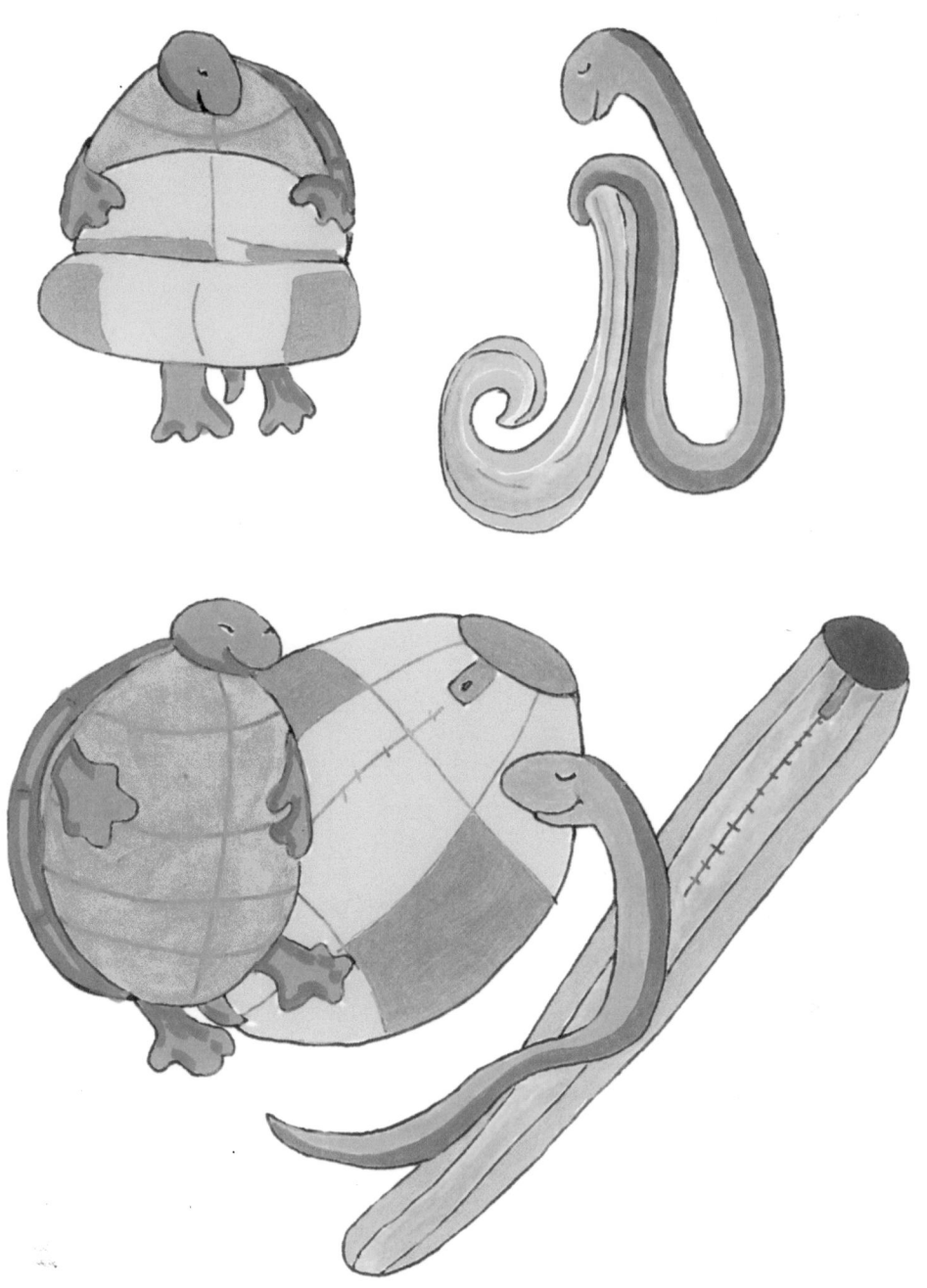

Out comes the food.

Whooo . . . Whooo

CAMP
MARSHMALLOWS

Run away!

Row, row across the pond.

Splash, splash in the brook.

March, march

around the trees.

There it is.

The perfect spot to camp.